Super Cat Speed!

Based on the screenplay
"Catboy's Great Gig"

Ready-to-Read

Simon Spotlight
New York   London   Toronto   Sydney   New Delhi

SIMON SPOTLIGHT
An imprint of Simon & Schuster Children's Publishing Division
1230 Avenue of the Americas, New York, New York 10020
This Simon Spotlight edition October 2020
Adapted by Cala Spinner from the series PJ Masks
All rights reserved, including the right of reproduction in whole or in part in any form.
SIMON SPOTLIGHT, READY-TO-READ, and colophon are registered trademarks of
Simon & Schuster, Inc.
For information about special discounts for bulk purchases, please contact
Simon & Schuster Special Sales at 1-866-506-1949 or business@simonandschuster.com.
Manufactured in the United States of America 0923 LAK
19
ISBN 978-1-5344-0927-9 (eBook)
ISBN 978-1-5344-9025-3 (prop)

The school concert

is tomorrow.

But where are

the instruments?

This is a job

for the PJ Masks!

Amaya becomes Owlette!

Greg becomes Gekko!

Connor becomes Catboy!

They are the PJ Masks!

Catboy is scared.

He does not want

to play in the concert.

What if he messes up?

The PJ Masks hear
a harsh noise.

It is Night Ninja!

Night Ninja is singing.

The Ninjalinos have
the missing instruments.

Catboy will use his
Super Cat Leap
to trap the Ninjalinos
with a net.

But he is too afraid.

It does not work.

"If we cannot get the instruments back, I guess the concert is off," says Owlette.

Catboy does not like
to see his friend sad.

Catboy uses Super Cat Speed!

He speeds around
the Ninjalinos.

He takes back one of
the instruments.

It is a recorder.

Catboy will need to
play the recorder.
Everyone is watching,
but Catboy must be brave.

Catboy plays the recorder.

He is really good!

The Ninjalinos like
playing with Catboy
more than Night Ninja.

They leave Night Ninja!

Then Owlette and Gekko
trap Night Ninja in a drum.

The Ninjalinos give
the instruments back.
"I will get you for this!"
Night Ninja says.

PJ Masks all shout hooray!

Because in the night,

we saved the day!

Catboy learned that
it is okay to be afraid,
but always do your best!